J

Soraya
&the Mermaid

ELR

by Salima Alikhan

illustrated by Atieh Sohrabi

"Estelle's Journey"
illustrated by Jennifer Naalchigar

Reycraft Books
55 Fifth Avenue
New York, NY 10003
Reycraftbooks.com

Reycraft Books is a trade imprint and trademark of Newmark Learning, LLC.

Library of Congress Control Number 2020908309

ISBN: 978-1-4788-6815-6

Author photo: Sam Bond Photography
Illustrator photos courtesy of Atieh Sohrabi and W.J. Naalchigar

Printed in Dongguan, China. 8557/0620/17230
10 9 8 7 6 5 4 3 2 1

First Edition Hardcover published by Reycraft Books

REYCRAFT
BOOKS

to Risa — S.A.

contents

Nimbla Moony

Nimbla Moony dipped and swooped through the clouds, tightly grasping onto her flying horse, Ziggy. "Faster, Ziggy!" she cried. "There isn't a moment to lose!"

Soraya could almost feel the breeze on her face and the tickle of the horse's mane blowing in the wind. Just then, Soraya's mom ruined everything by striding into the kitchen. Quick as a flash, Soraya slipped *Nimbla Moony and the Rescue Mission* behind her back.

"What are you reading, Soraya?" her mom asked, pouring herself some coffee.

"Nothing." Soraya shifted in her seat as she pushed around bits of egg on her plate.

"Is it those comic books again? It's that Mimbla Noomy character, isn't it?"

"*Nimbla Moony*," Soraya said loudly. Then she muttered, "I bet Nimbla Moony never had to eat eggs, *ever.*"

"Stop playing with your food, and cheer up. Your field trip today will be a blast. You always loved the aquarium when you were little."

"Back then I thought all the fish were aliens," Soraya said, squishing her eggs with a fork. "Now I'm ten, and I know they're just from the ocean. Plus, back then I didn't have to go with my class."

"What's so bad about your class?" Her mom put down her coffee cup.

Soraya opened her mouth to say that real people were boring, not like the characters in comic books. Instead she said, "I told you before, Mom. My whole class thinks I'm a weirdo."

Her mother pressed her mouth into a thin line. It was the "I'm-disappointed-and-I'm-not-even-trying-to-hide-it" face.

"Well, maybe if you stopped ignoring them, they wouldn't think that."

Soraya rolled her eyes. Moms had no clue. Why couldn't she have Nimbla Moony's life? Nimbla had hatched out of a magical egg on the planet Zybon. Therefore she had zero experience with annoying parents.

"Anyway," her mom said, "being different is a good thing."

How would you *know?* Soraya thought. But Soraya didn't say that either. She remembered all the sideways looks the other kids gave her. Or they would say, "You're so *weird*, Soraya."

Like the time Lola was crying because she had gotten a bad grade. Soraya told Lola to do what Nimbla Moony recommended—hold a funeral for the bad grade, at the Bad Grade Graveyard. On the moon.

This didn't go over very well with Lola. She had avoided Soraya ever since.

Another time, Frankie had said he was scared of the dark. Soraya suggested he try asking the ghost of his dead guinea pig to protect him.

That time, Frankie's mother had called Soraya's mother to complain that Soraya had given her son nightmares.

How could her mom possibly understand what it was like to be the weirdest kid in fourth grade? Soraya's mom was exceedingly normal. She had a normal job and wore normal beige clothes and said normal things.

Soraya scooted around on her chair.

"You know, Mom, Nimbla Moony doesn't even bother with people. She mostly talks to her horse."

"I don't want your hero to be a comic book character who mostly talks to a horse," Soraya's mother said, carrying their dishes to the sink. "I want you to make a friend who is a *real person*. Maybe you can try that on this aquarium trip?"

"I doubt it," Soraya mumbled.

When Soraya looked up, she felt guilty. Her mom was trying to hide it, but she was wearing the worst face of all. The worried face.

"Go finish getting ready for school. And, Soraya, don't take any comic books with you."

Soraya shoved her bag lunch into her backpack and ran up to her room to get some pencils. She stopped in front of her dresser. There was an old framed photo of Soraya and her parents from when she was in kindergarten.

It was strange to see her dad smiling. That wasn't how Soraya remembered him. He had left her and her mom years ago. Before he left, he had frowned an awful lot. At *her*.

"What are we going to do with you, Soraya?" he would say.

Soraya knew exactly what *that* meant. It was a grown-up's way of saying, *You're so weird.*

Soraya's fists clenched. She hadn't talked to her dad in years. Even her mom didn't know where he was.

Her mom told Soraya it wasn't her fault that her dad had left. Sometimes it was hard to believe that, though. She wanted to throw the photo across the room.

"Almost ready, Soraya?" her mom called out.

Soraya grabbed two of her favorite *Nimbla Moony* comics. She rolled them up and stuffed them into her backpack.

She felt better right away.

"I'm coming!"

"Soraya, hurry up, or you're going to miss the bus to the field trip!" her mom yelled. If only she could be that lucky.

When her mom dropped her off at school, Soraya leafed through a comic book as the class waited together outside the building. It was the foggiest day she could remember.

A big yellow bus pulled up with its engine rumbling. Her classmates rushed up the steps, laughing and chattering loudly about the animals they were going to see at the aquarium. Soraya climbed up behind them onto the crowded, noisy bus.

Whenever she was around a lot of people, Soraya imagined an invisible force field going up in front of her body. *"Shields engaged,"* she whispered to herself.

She squeezed her way down the aisle. The windows were misted over from the fog, and kids were using their fingers to draw animals on the glass.

"A hammerhead shark looks like *this*," Chesney was shouting. He drew a squiggly blob on the window. Soraya thought it looked nothing like a shark.

She plopped down in the very last seat.

"Hey, Soraya," said a voice. "Do you want to sit with us?"

It was Naomi. She was standing right in front of Soraya.

"Oh," said Soraya. She couldn't think of anything to say.

"Uh . . . no, it's okay," Soraya finally said, clearing her throat. "The back of the bus is a good, um, defensive position. You never know when we might be attacked by aliens."

"What?" said Naomi.

Soraya looked down. "I just mean . . . you don't have to ask me to sit with you. You don't need to feel sorry for me." She blushed and turned to the window.

Naomi's shoulders dropped. "Well, okay. Come up if you change your mind."

Soraya watched Naomi go back to her friends, her dark curly ponytail bouncing as she walked. Soraya felt a pang in the middle of her chest. She wanted to join them.

But she knew that if she went up there, it would be about three seconds before someone said, *You're so weird, Soraya.*

Soraya slumped down so no one else would see her and feel sorry for her. She drew her own shark in the window. *Hers* looked really good. Soraya was so busy drawing that she barely noticed when the bus pulled up in front of Bayside Aquarium.

The Face in the Tank

The class spilled out of the bus. Excited voices rose higher and higher.

"Please stay together, everyone!" called their teacher, Ms. Staples, as they poured into the aquarium building.

"Welcome to Bayside Aquarium," said a young woman standing by the front doors. "I'm going to pass out wristbands so that we know you all belong together."

"I want to see the beluga whales," said Phong.

"The otters are my favorite," said Lupita.

"No way—the hippos!" said Christoff.

"Christoff," said Katie, "what kind of *pants* are you wearing?"

Katie was making a scrunched-up face that Soraya had seen a million times. Usually, Katie made that face at Soraya. It made her feel like pulling Katie's hair, hard.

"They're lederhosen," said Christoff. He stood up straight and patted the suspenders attached to his short brown pants. "They're from Germany. I've wanted a pair forever, and my mom finally got me some.

So, which animals do you want to see?"

Katie shrugged. "The sea turtles, I guess."

"Some people think turtles are descended from sea serpents, so be careful," Soraya heard herself say, before she could pull the words back into her mouth.

Everyone nearby stared at her.

"Are you serious?" Katie asked with a giggle.

Soraya shifted from foot to foot. She knew the normal thing to do was to smile and say she was just kidding. But she wasn't kidding.

"You're so *weird*, Soraya," said Katie, still giggling.

Soraya almost reached out to pull Katie's hair, but just then another aquarium worker appeared. He guided the kids over to the tide pool tank, which had starfish, sea cucumbers, and hermit crabs in shallow water.

"You may touch the animals gently," he said.

Everyone except Soraya crowded around the low sides of the tank and plunged their hands into the water.

The aquarium worker came over to Soraya. "Would you like to try the tide pool?" he asked.

The only spot left was next to Katie. Soraya shook her head. No way, no how. Soraya's chest went tight. She had to get away, even if it was just for a minute.

Soraya saw a sign that read "This way to the Ocean Journey exhibit." She took her chance and zipped into the hallway. It was like a see-through tube through a huge fish tank. Sharks and stingrays swam by over her head, their bellies just feet above her.

She walked out into a large room and took a deep breath. It was as empty and quiet as the planet Hush, where Nimbla Moony went to rest after her adventures.

The Ocean Journey tank was so big that the water inside seemed to disappear up into the ceiling. The bigger fish drifted by, in no rush at all. Some of them were three times as long as Soraya. Shimmering schools of smaller fish darted around.

What did fish think about? Were they jealous that people had legs? Or did they feel sorry for people, with their chunky, awkward feet? Nimbla Moony would know what the fish were thinking. She could read animals' minds.

"Hey, fish," Soraya called out. "You guys look like you're having fun. Is it as fun as it looks?"

One of the oddest-looking fish she'd ever seen was walking sideways along the tank's floor. It had huge bright red lips, and it seemed to look right at Soraya. A sign next to the tank said it was a red-lipped batfish.

"Can't you swim, or do you have to walk?" she asked as the fish scuttled by. She pointed at the other fish. "They better not be mean to you for being different."

Just then, Soraya thought she saw something move in a cave-like hole under some coral.

And then a *face* appeared in the hole. It couldn't be—*a human face*!

Soraya jumped back. Before she could scream, even more of the person wriggled out of the coral. She could see the whole top half of the person's body.

Soraya clapped her hands to her mouth.

It was a girl. Inside the tank, with the sharks and other fish. She had dark skin and wore a bathing suit top. Her curly black hair swirled like clouds in the water.

"Shh! Don't give me away," said the girl, holding a finger to her lips. The sound was a little muffled, but Soraya could hear her clearly through the glass.

The girl looked terrified. What was she doing in the Ocean Journey tank? Why didn't she have a wetsuit and scuba gear? And why in the world was she under the coral?

Soraya was breathing hard and fast. She tried to calm herself down. *What would Nimbla Moony do?*

Nimbla would come to the rescue, if a rescue was needed.

"Did you fall into the tank?" Soraya asked.

The girl shook her head. Then she wriggled the rest of the way out of the coral.

Soraya sucked in a breath. She tried hard to remind herself that Nimbla Moony never panicked.

But what Soraya saw made her PANIC.

The top of the girl's body was human. But the bottom half was . . . a *fish.*

A shiny, green-blue fish that glimmered in the light.

"Don't scream," the girl begged.

Soraya staggered backward. She tried to make sense of it. All her brain came up with was that this girl had dressed up like a mermaid. Then she must have jumped into the tank to get attention.

If that was the case, Soraya had finally met someone weirder than she was.

The girl came right up to the glass. "Don't tell anyone I'm here!" she said. It seemed that the girl didn't want attention after all.

And then, just as suddenly as she had appeared, the girl dove back into the cave under the coral.

Soraya turned around. Two people had walked in to see the Ocean Journey exhibit. Soraya held her breath as they walked past her.

Then she looked back at the tank. The girl poked her face out again, just enough for Soraya to see.

So Soraya hadn't imagined her.

Soraya checked to make sure the other people in the room weren't watching or listening. They were busy talking to each other and looking at the red-lipped batfish.

"How can you hold your breath for so long under water?" asked Soraya. "I've never heard of anyone who can do that."

The girl just pointed at the bottom half of her body—that costume tail, or whatever it was. Then she pointed up to the top of the tank.

"Can you meet me up there? At the top of the water?"

Soraya glanced around the room. "I don't know where the top of the tank is. I can't get up there by myself."

The girl's face fell. "You have to," she said. "My life depends on it." And then she dove back into the coral cave.

Soraya's legs were shaking so hard she had to sit down on the bench. The other people in the room had left. She couldn't believe what had just happened. A girl had jumped into the fish tank and wanted *Soraya* to get her out.

It wasn't every day that someone asked her to rescue them. Nimbla Moony might be the galaxy's best rescuer, but Soraya decided that she could be the second best.

Soraya straightened her shoulders and raced out of the room.

To the Rescue

Soraya left the Ocean Journey exhibit by a door on the far side of the room. She looked around for clues that might tell her how to get to the top of the aquarium tank.

A few feet down this hallway was a staircase. The fish-girl had been pointing upward. It made sense that the top of the tank would be upstairs.

She ran toward the staircase, and almost bumped into an aquarium worker as he came down the steps. It was an elderly man.

"Hello," he said, squinting at her. He pointed at her purple bracelet. "You're here with a group? Where are they?"

"I'm on a rescue mission!" Soraya declared.

The man leaned forward and looked at her with suspicion. "You're on a WHAT? I'm hard of hearing."

"Oh. Um . . . " said Soraya. She realized just in time that Nimbla wouldn't give herself away. She would act like a spy and make up a story. "I said, I'm with my class," Soraya blurted out loudly. "I just went to the bathroom and now I'm going to join them again."

The man nodded and turned to go. Soraya pretended to walk the other way. But as soon as the man was gone, she raced back to the staircase and ran up the steps.

At the top of the stairs was a sign that read "STAFF ONLY." She slowly cracked the door open. It led into a long hallway with lots of doors. She smelled coffee. At the end of the hall, three adults were talking and holding mugs.

Soraya's heart thudded. She quietly snuck across the hallway and hid behind a corner. Then she stuck her head out, watching them.

In this situation, Nimbla Moony would probably stop the grown-ups in their tracks with her freeze ray.

Soraya couldn't do that. Maybe she could pull the fire alarm to get them to leave, though. Just as she was about to try it, the grown-ups started walking away. They stepped onto an elevator at the other end of the hall.

Soraya sighed with relief. She started tiptoe-running down the hall, reading all the different signs on the doors. One sign said "Jellyfish." Another said "Veterinarian."

Finally she came to a door that was marked "Ocean Journey." She pushed it open. It was definitely the right room. It was bigger than the

gym at her school, with a high ceiling and lots of tanks and other equipment.

And in the very middle of it was something that looked like a gigantic swimming pool.

Soraya tiptoed over. It wasn't a pool, of course—it was the top of the Ocean Journey tank. Stingrays and sharks swam by slowly in the water.

Soraya peered down into the tank, hoping none of the sharks would jump out and bite her face off. She didn't see the girl anywhere.

She stood up and glanced around the empty room. Someone would probably come in any second. Soraya would get in big trouble. They'd take her back to her class and Ms. Staples would call Soraya's mother. And then Soraya's life would basically be over.

She turned to leave, then glanced back at the water one more time.

A small, worried face was swimming up toward her.

Soraya's heart beat like crazy when she saw the girl's shiny fish tail. It swished behind her, pushing the girl up through the water.

The girl's head popped up out of the water. She was small, no bigger than Soraya. She splashed over to the side of the tank.

"Who . . . *what* are you?" Soraya asked.

The girl's eyes were round and dark. Drops of water shone all over her dark brown skin, and wet black curls hung down her back. "What do you mean?" she said.

"You can hold your breath for a really long time," Soraya said, her voice shaking. "And . . . how did you get that tail on? Is it a Halloween costume or something?"

The girl lifted the end of her tail up out of the water. It was the most realistic costume tail Soraya had ever seen. The scales glistened exactly like a fish.

Soraya moved closer. It seemed impossible, but where the girl's tail ended at her waist, the scales blended right into her skin. They became *part* of her skin.

Soraya had never seen a costume like that.

She felt dizzy. It couldn't be true. Nothing exciting ever happened to her. Her life was eggs in the morning, avoiding people at school, and homework and reading at night. Over and over again. Pretty boring. All the exciting stuff happened to Nimbla Moony.

"I'm a mermaid." The girl floated with ease at the top of the tank.

Soraya sat down at the edge of the tank. She pinched herself, hard. "*Ow.*"

"Why did you do that?" asked the mermaid girl, as a red mark appeared on Soraya's arm.

Soraya rubbed at the mark. "To make sure I'm not dreaming."

"I'm real," said the girl. "My name's Estelle. What's yours?"

"Soraya," Soraya answered. The girl looked blank, so she added, "It means 'star' in Persian. It can mean 'jewel' too, but I like 'star' better."

"You humans have so many languages," Estelle said with a sigh. "My people try to learn as many human languages as we can. We're always worried we'll have to deal with humans one day, so we like to prepare."

"Who's 'we'?" asked Soraya. "There are more fish-people?"

"Merpeople," Estelle corrected her.

"So you live . . . ?" Soraya pointed at the tank.

Estelle looked down into the water. "Do I live *here*? Oh gosh, no. I'm from the ocean. That's where all merpeople are from."

One of the enormous manta rays swam right up to the surface next to them. Soraya jumped back, but the ray gave Estelle's hand a friendly nudge, as if it were a puppy. Then it dove back down into the depths of the tank.

Soraya's head was spinning. "How did you end up here?" she asked.

"Some fishing boats were out catching small fish to feed the aquarium animals, and I got caught in the net," said Estelle.

"Didn't the people on the boat see you?" asked Soraya.

"Luckily, no," said Estelle. "I managed to hide in a big clump of seaweed and got dumped into a holding tank. I found my way into the Ocean Journey tank, and I've been hiding here ever since."

Estelle sighed. "I've got to get back. Everyone in my kingdom is worried about me, I'm sure."

"You have a *kingdom*?" said Soraya weakly, leaning on the side of the tank.

"Well, I'm not the leader of it if that's what you mean," said the mermaid. "But yes, I live in a kingdom. Under the sea. Speaking of my kingdom—I need to get back there as soon as possible. Can you help me?"

Soraya was glad she was already sitting down, because she felt as if she might faint.

The Yellow Bucket

ou—you want *me* to get you out of here?" said Soraya, alarmed. "Why don't you just ask the people from the aquarium to let you go?"

Estelle snorted. "Are you kidding me? I know what humans do when they find an 'interesting species.' They lock them up and study them."

She frowned. "They'll do experiments on me. And then they'll send divers to hunt for my people."

Soraya thought about all the movies she'd ever seen about strange creatures coming into the human world. She had to agree. The aquarium scientists probably wouldn't let Estelle go back to the ocean.

Estelle patted a ray as it swam by. "Every fish in this tank is telling me to get out of here as fast as I can."

Soraya stared into the water. "The *fish* have been telling you that?"

"Yeah. They're my friends."

Of course they were. Soraya's mind reeled.

"Why did you show yourself to me, if you're trying to hide?" Soraya asked.

"You walked right up to the glass and started talking to the fish, like you respect them," said Estelle. "And you were alone, without a grown-up. I knew an adult would give me away."

Estelle lowered her voice. "Are human adults as grumpy as they always look?"

"Yeah, pretty much," said Soraya.

"So, can you help me get back to the ocean?" asked Estelle.

"Me?" said Soraya. "There's no way I could get you out of here without people seeing us."

Estelle's face fell.

"There must be *something* we can do," said Estelle. She sounded scared.

Soraya started shivering. Nimbla Moony never shivered when someone needed rescuing. Clearly Soraya was not as brave as Nimbla.

But as Soraya shivered, she looked around. Her eyes landed on a janitor's bucket nearby—a wide yellow bucket with wheels and a handle you could push or pull.

Maybe . . .

Suddenly, there was a noise at the door.

Estelle dove back into the water. She was gone before Soraya could blink. Soraya raced behind a big water pump and peeked out.

A woman came into the room. She was carrying scuba gear—a wetsuit, goggles, flippers, and an oxygen tank. She walked past Soraya's hiding place and went through a door marked "Restroom." Soraya raced back to the water.

Estelle was waiting just a few feet below the surface. When she saw Soraya, she swam back up to the edge of the tank.

"I think that was one of the scuba divers who goes in to clean the tank," Soraya said breathlessly. "She just went into the bathroom. She must be putting on her wetsuit."

Estelle glanced at the bathroom door. "I hate when divers come into the tank," she whispered. "I have to curl up and hide under the coral the whole time."

"We have to get you out of here before she comes back!" Soraya tried to ignore her own terror as she ran and grabbed the big yellow janitor's bucket. Luckily, it was empty. She dragged it back to the pool. "Get in here."

Estelle looked at the bucket suspiciously. "What's that?"

"It's a bucket," said Soraya. "Get in, quick."

"Where will you take me?"

Soraya thought a minute. "The bay is right across the street."

"Yes!" Estelle said. "The bay will take me to the ocean!"

"Okay," said Soraya. Her mouth felt dry. She couldn't believe she was even thinking about doing this. If they were caught, Estelle might be locked up in some laboratory, and it would be all Soraya's fault.

"Are you all right?" said Estelle.

Soraya gulped. "Sure. So . . . all we have to do is sneak you out of the aquarium and across the street to the bay."

"Let's do it!" said Estelle, her eyes shining.

Soraya glanced at the bathroom door. If Nimbla Moony were there, she would freeze time so that they could escape without the diver noticing. But, again, Soraya didn't have that choice. "Hurry, *get in the bucket!*"

"Uh, how?" asked Estelle. "I can't exactly climb in, and you don't look strong enough to pick me up."

"Try this." Soraya laid the bucket down on its side. "Come out of the water and crawl in here. Once you're in it, I'll tip the bucket back up."

"This is going to be *very* awkward," said Estelle, pulling herself out of the water. She plopped to the floor and started wriggling toward the bucket. She looked like a girl-sized inchworm.

Soraya hoped it would take a long time for the scuba diver to put on her wetsuit.

"Can't you go any faster?" she whispered.

"You try this without legs," Estelle whispered back as she tried to pull herself into the bucket. "I'm doing my best."

"Okay, okay. Maybe you could turn around and get in tail-first?" said Soraya.

"I think I can sit in the bucket with my tail hanging out," Estelle said. "Can you help me?"

Soraya grabbed Estelle's hands as Estelle bent at the waist and wiggled into the bucket.

"Now hold on tight." Soraya tugged at the bucket. It was harder than she thought it would be. She pushed with all her might. Estelle held on to the sides of the bucket and squeezed her eyes shut.

Finally, the bucket lurched back onto its wheels with a loud *clunk*.

Soraya was sure the diver must have heard that. She grabbed the handle of the bucket and started racing for the door, the bucket rolling behind her.

"I think I'm land-sick," said Estelle.

"*Sshhhh!*" Soraya hissed.

The doors were only a few feet away when the restroom door creaked open behind them.

Soraya turned around and froze. She didn't move as the woman looked toward the pool.

"Hello?" the diver called. "Is someone here?"

48

Elevator Down

Just as the diver was about to turn toward Soraya and Estelle, one of the stingrays leapt out of the tank in a graceful arc. It looked as if it were flying. Then it splashed back down again, spraying water everywhere.

A second later, another ray did the same. Waves sloshed over the sides of the tank. More stingrays joined in, jumping out of the water one after another. "What's wrong with you all?" the diver cried, rushing over to the tank.

"They're distracting her," Estelle whispered, "so we can get out of here. Hurry!"

Soraya dragged the bucket toward the doors. Behind them, the diver was still trying to figure out why the rays were acting so strangely.

A few seconds later, she and Estelle were out the door.

"Fish make loyal friends," said Estelle breathlessly. "I knew Bert and Elaine and the others would help."

Soraya leaned against the wall, panting. "There are stingrays called *Bert* and *Elaine*?"

Before Estelle could answer, there was a noise from the other end of the hall. Soraya whipped around. She heard muffled voices, and they were getting closer. People were coming up the same staircase she'd climbed earlier.

Soraya grabbed the handle of the bucket again. "Hold tight!"

She raced for the elevator, pulling Estelle behind her. The mermaid kept making terrified yelps, but Soraya didn't slow down until they reached the end of the hall. She punched the "down" button over and over, glancing down the hall every two seconds.

It felt like the doors took a hundred years to slide open. As soon as they did, Soraya shoved Estelle's bucket into the elevator and followed. Once the doors slid closed, she leaned against the wall. Her heart was hammering.

"Why are we in this box?" Estelle said in a small voice. Her bright scaly tail curled over the side of the bucket, and water dripped onto the elevator floor. Now *she* was shivering.

"Oh—it's an elevator." Soraya wiped the sweat off her forehead. "It moves up and down and takes you to different floors of a building." Soraya leaned against the elevator wall, but she didn't hit the button for the first floor. She needed time to think. She was starting to realize that her plan was impossible.

"How wonderful!" exclaimed Estelle. "I will have to find out how an elevator works. Then I can include elevators in some of the buildings I'm designing."

Soraya shook her head. "Wait, what buildings?"

"Where I come from, the buildings are all crooked or falling apart," said Estelle. That's because merpeople don't value math or architects. They're more interested in art and dancing. I design buildings that can stand up to harsh ocean conditions. I'm going to start building them soon. They'll last for centuries."

"You design *buildings*?" said Soraya. "But— you look like you're the same age as me, and I'm only ten!"

Estelle's looked confused. "Yes, I'm ten. So?"

"How did you learn?" said Soraya. "And your parents—they just let you design real buildings?"

"I've been reading and teaching myself about math and architecture," Estelle explained. "And merpeople stop telling their kids what to do when we're really small. Don't your parents let you do what you want?"

"My mom doesn't." Soraya fiddled with an elevator button. "And my father . . ."

Her cheeks burned. Soraya never talked about her dad. But for some reason she added, "He might as well live on another planet. Sometimes I think I'm an alien who hatched out of an egg."

Estelle's tail flicked. "I feel really different from my family, too. They've never supported my work."

Soraya blinked at her. "But your friends support you, right?"

Estelle shrugged. "I don't really have friends— well, except fish. Like I said, architecture isn't very popular with merpeople." She set her jaw. "But I *will* change their minds. I know it."

Soraya thought about telling Estelle that she didn't have any friends, either. But she stopped herself. Right now, Estelle was looking at her as if she was a completely normal person.

"Nimbla Moony likes outcasts," Soraya said. "All her friends are outcasts."

"Who's Nimbla Moony?" asked Estelle. She actually looked interested.

"Oh . . . she's a comic book superhero." Soraya patted her backpack and felt the rolled-up comics through the fabric. "She says outcasts are the most interesting people."

"Well, some people might call me an outcast. That doesn't matter," said Estelle. "I know my ideas and plans are important." She glanced at the elevator panel. "But I won't ever get to build anything unless I get back to the ocean."

Estelle was getting colder. She shivered so hard the bucket shook.

Soraya took her jacket out of her backpack and gave it to Estelle.

"Nimbla Moony would cover you with her extra-warm bubble cape. But this jacket is the best I can do."

"Where is the elevator taking us, anyway?" said Estelle.

"To the entrance hall, once I press this button. But it might be really crowded down there. I have no idea how we'll hide you. *Everyone* will see us. I don't know *what* to do." Soraya put her hands on her head.

"What's an entrance hall?" asked Estelle.

"It's the front part of the aquarium, a big room where people come in," said Soraya.

"I can scrunch down. Maybe no one will see me," Estelle offered, curling up her tail in the bucket.

"This bucket isn't big enough. Plus, it would

still look weird for me to be pulling a janitor's bucket around, whether people can see you or not," said Soraya. "Everyone would think I'm even weirder than they already d—"

She stopped herself just in time.

"Everyone would think what?" said Estelle.

"Nothing," Soraya said quickly.

"So what are we going to do?" asked Estelle.

"I don't know," Soraya admitted. "But we should go down, in case anyone tries to get on this elevator. We've been in here a while already."

Soraya's hand shook as she pushed the button for the first floor. The elevator gave a lurch and then started moving slowly. Estelle's eyes widened with surprise and she gripped the bucket tighter.

The elevator bell dinged. They both gulped.

"We're here!" Soraya said.

Unexpected Help

"We'll just peek out." Soraya tried to sound confident and in charge. "So we can figure out where to hide."

The doors slid open on the first floor. Soraya shoved Estelle's bucket as far as she could into the corner of the elevator and out of sight. Then she peered out.

Her heart sank. She realized she had gotten mixed up—this elevator was far away from the entrance hall. In fact, it was all the way on the other side of the building from where Soraya's class had come in. There were lots of exhibits between here and the front doors.

At least there were fewer people around than she expected.

Across the room, a couple of families were gathered around the tanks. A father carried a little girl on his shoulders. Another dad lifted his little boy to look into the otter exhibit.

Soraya felt a twinge in her gut. This was no time to be distracted by twinges, but she couldn't help it. She didn't like seeing normal dads with their normal kids—kids whose dads stuck around.

Soraya jutted out her lip. Who needed to be *normal*, anyway? Nimbla Moony was just fine not being normal, and she had the most fun of anyone in the whole galaxy.

"Soraya," whispered Estelle. "Are you paying attention? What's our plan?"

"What? Oh, sorry." Soraya waited until the people had walked past the elevator. Then she grabbed the bucket's handle. "Let's go!"

"Careful, careful," Estelle murmured as Soraya pushed the bucket as fast as she could toward a large column near the closest tank.

Once they were wedged between the column and the huge tank, Soraya looked out again. Her heart was hammering. She couldn't believe they'd made it even a few feet without being discovered. She and Estelle were hidden for now, but as soon as people came toward them, they'd be seen for sure.

Soraya studied the long area between their hiding place and the entrance hall.

"We have to figure out how to get you through all those exhibits without anyone noticing us," she said desperately, thinking about the distance they would have to cover. "If we can make it to the entrance hall, then we have to get *through* the hall to the front doors. There are guards standing at the doors. We'll have to get past them somehow, too."

Soraya pressed herself against the column. What had she done? She should have left Estelle in the tank and tried to figure out another way. She was going to get them both arrested. Estelle would spend the rest of her life in a special mermaid jail.

Soraya turned around and almost screamed.

A face was pressed up against the inside of the tank behind her. It was a huge gray face, with big eyes and a humongous snout.

Behind the gray face, a gigantic gray body floated in the water. A smaller gray body floated next to the big one.

It was a mama and baby hippo! Soraya had forgotten all about the hippos. They must have come in from their outdoor area.

The mama hippo blinked down at Estelle.

"Sister," it said, "what are you doing there?"

Soraya almost screamed again.

"It's—it's talking!" she said, gasping and backing up against the column.

"Of course she's talking," said Estelle, thumping Soraya's arm. "*Ssshhh*. Animals are always talking."

"Well, I don't usually hear them," Soraya said.

"They're very picky about who they talk to," said Estelle. "They don't talk in front of just anyone."

Soraya stared at the mama hippo. Her eyes looked as intelligent as any person's eyes.

"Humans." The hippo rolled her eyes, shook her head, and turned to Estelle. "Do you need help? It looks like you have a dilemma."

"What's a dilemma?" asked Soraya.

"It's a problem," said the hippo. "I'm assuming you two have a problem. After all, you're hiding behind a column and one of you is sitting in a janitor's bucket."

Soraya felt herself blush. She stood up straight. "I've got it under control," she said. "*I'm* rescuing Estelle."

The hippo didn't look impressed. "Sure," she said. She turned and nodded at the baby hippo. Then they both started swimming back and forth in the tank.

"What are you doing?" asked Soraya, alarmed.

"Helping," said the hippo. "You'll see."

"We don't need any help." Soraya moved in front of Estelle's bucket. "I told you, I've got everything under control."

"Soraya, look!" Estelle squealed.

A group of aquarium visitors had just come around the corner. They were walking right toward Soraya and Estelle's hiding place.

"Don't move yet," said the mama hippo in a low voice. She and the baby swam to the other end of the tank, closer to the people.

One of the kids in the group stopped before he reached the column that Soraya and Estelle were hiding behind. He pointed at the tank and screamed, "Mom, *look!*"

"Whoa," said one of the grown-ups in the group. "Come here, guys! This is amazing!"

Soraya peeked back at the tank. The hippos were *dancing*. Mama and baby hippo spun and glided in the water, their legs paddling

gracefully beneath their huge bellies. It looked as if they weighed nothing at all.

People's faces lit up as they streamed over to look at the hippos.

The baby hippo was flipping like crazy. The mother hippo did a graceful twirl.

"They're making people look away from us. Let's go!" Estelle said.

Soraya stared. "Oh. Oh yeah!" She grabbed the bucket's handle and zoomed out from the other side of the column. The people in the group were too busy to notice them as they raced away. But Soraya realized they couldn't make it all the way to the entrance hall. There were too many people around.

She yanked Estelle into the next hiding place she could see: a huge potted plant, with thick leaves that fanned out everywhere.

"Okay," Soraya panted, her heart racing.

She pushed the bucket in among the blanket of leaves. The plant was a way better hiding place than the column had been. She let out a deep breath.

"I wish this bucket weren't so *yellow*," she muttered. "It stands out everywhere."

"Where are we now?" said Estelle, leaning out of the bucket.

Before Soraya could answer, she heard a voice say, "Hey, Christoff, could you tell me where to get a pair of those lederhosen?"

Soraya felt like her heart had stopped. She recognized that voice.

It was Naomi.

She peeked out from behind the plant. Her whole class was just twenty feet away.

Underwater Opera

Soraya shrank down behind the plant and made a strangled sound.

"That noise means something bad, right?" Estelle asked.

"Yes," Soraya said, gasping for air. "That's my *class* over there."

Estelle peered out from behind the leaves. "I think I've read about that," she said. "A class is a group of people you go to school with, right?"

"Uh, right." said Soraya, surprised. She paused. "You sit in a room and learn together. Don't you go to school?"

"We learn mostly from our parents," Estelle said. "Or we study on our own. I heard that humans get to have school *all day.*" She sighed. "I'm so jealous."

"Why?" said Soraya, watching her class. They were still milling around; she and Estelle would just have to wait until they left. "Who wishes they could go to *school?*"

Estelle shook her head. "If I went to school, I'd study architecture every day. I'd even have people to study with." She peeked out at Soraya's class again. "Which ones are your friends?"

Soraya coughed. "Oh. My friends? All of them. Every single one. They're all my friends. I'm very popular."

Estelle sighed. "That must be so nice."

"Don't you have at least one friend where you live?" Soraya asked.

Estelle shook her head. "No one except Gregory. He's an octopus, a smart one. When I start building my city, he'll help."

"What about your parents?" said Soraya.

"They're proud of me, but they don't care about my buildings," said Estelle. "They both wish I would just be a normal mermaid who likes singing and underwater dancing. I told them they'll thank me when I build them an earthquake-proof house."

Estelle picked at a dead leaf on the plant. "What about your mother? Does she support your work?"

Soraya hesitated. "I don't have work, not like that. Most, um, human fourth graders don't."

"That's sad," said Estelle, studying her. "But at least you have friends. I'd love to have friends to talk to."

"Yeah. Well," said Soraya, "if I lived in the ocean, I'd hang out with you and help you build earthquake-proof houses."

Estelle brightened. "And if I lived here, I'd go to your class and read about Mimble Moony with you." She paused thoughtfully. "Except I'd probably have to sit in a bucket."

Soraya couldn't help it: she started laughing. Soon Estelle was laughing too. Soraya knew there was no time for silliness, but they both kept laughing and laughing. They laughed so hard that they tried to muffle their giggles by sticking their faces into the plant's leaves.

This is what it's like to have a friend, thought Soraya. Suddenly she remembered what her mom had said at breakfast: "I want you to make a friend who is a *real person*." What would she say if she knew about *this* friend, a magical fish-girl with a long, shiny tail? Soraya laughed even harder.

Estelle wiped her eyes, still hiccuping with laughter. She pointed out at the exhibits. "We're going to have to ask the other animals to help us, too, like the hippos did."

"*No!*" Soraya turned to her. "We don't need help. *I'll* get you out of here."

Soraya held on tight to the handle of the bucket. Rescuing Estelle was the most important thing she'd ever done. It might even be the only *good* thing she'd ever done. If she was going to keep her new friend, she needed to prove she could protect her, and that she wouldn't leave her. Soraya thought about her father, and how he had left. She wouldn't do that to Estelle.

"Why don't you want to ask for help?" Estelle asked. "I think we'll need it. Hey—maybe you can ask your friends to help us, too."

Soraya swallowed. "My friends?"

"Yeah—your friends in your class. Would they help us escape?"

Soraya fidgeted. "Uh . . . I don't know. I don't want to get them in trouble."

Estelle looked disappointed. "All right. Then I'll ask the animals."

Before Soraya could stop her, Estelle leaned out from behind the plant and waved her arms wildly at the nearest tank—the beluga whales.

Soraya had never paid much attention to beluga whales before. Now she noticed how friendly they looked. There were three of them swimming in the water, smiling down at Soraya and Estelle. Soraya wondered how long they'd been watching.

"We need a distraction," Estelle told them, leaning so far out of the bucket that Soraya was afraid she'd fall out. "We have to get across the exhibit without anyone seeing us. She's taking me back to the sea."

The whales kept swimming. They didn't seem to be in any rush.

"It's odd to see a human helping one of our kind," one whale remarked. "Odd but nice."

"I am not *odd*," Soraya said, leaning over Estelle to scowl at them.

"Oh, dear," said the whale. "I'm so sorry if I offended. I just meant—"

"You're taking her back to the sea?" the middle whale interrupted, beaming at Soraya. "How lovely! Your parents must be so proud. A brave, strange human like you helping a friend."

Soraya couldn't hold back a growl. "I am *not strange*. I am *completely and totally average*!"

She didn't want someone calling her strange in front of Estelle. Not while Estelle still thought Soraya was normal.

Estelle changed the subject. "Can you help us, please?" she asked the whales. "And quickly?"

"We'll help," said one of the whales, bobbing his head, "but the problem is, we're not sure about the song choice."

"*What*?" said Soraya.

The second whale shook his head. "If only we had time to compose something."

"It doesn't matter, really," said Estelle. "Please just help us!"

The whales nodded and swam to the other side of the tank. A moment later one of the most beautiful sounds Soraya had ever heard filled the room.

The whales were *singing*. In harmony.

"Oh my gosh—listen!" yelped Christoff. Hopping in excitement in his lederhosen, he ran over to the whales. Naomi followed. Soon the rest of the class ran up, too.

The three whales swam side by side in the tank, serenading the people.

Even Ms. Staples looked wonderstruck. "I had no idea belugas could sing like that," she said to a nearby aquarium worker. The young man stood there with his mouth open wide. "I didn't either," he said.

By now, Soraya's whole class was plastered to the glass of the whales' tank. People were coming from all over the area to stare and listen.

"We should go now," said Estelle.

Soraya gripped the handle of the bucket and looked around for another hiding place closer to the entrance hall. The best thing she saw was a large sign standing in front of the otter exhibit.

She bolted out from behind the plant, dragging the bucket behind her. She ducked behind the sign and made sure Estelle was tucked safely out of sight.

"Look, the entrance hall's right over there," Soraya said—just as a cold stream of water hit her in the face.

She looked up, sputtering. The beady black eyes of an otter peered at her over the side of the exhibit, which was an open space with a pool. Through the clear glass of the tank, she could see otters zooming though the water.

"I heard you'd be coming," the otter said in a fast, breathless voice. "Word travels fast. Got yourselves in a fix, I see?"

"No," said Soraya, angrily brushing water from her face. "We're *fine*. We don't need any—"

"Soraya, why do you keep telling them we don't need help?" said Estelle, twisting around in the bucket to look at Soraya. She sounded annoyed for the first time. "We need all the help we can get. I have to get back home before the aquarium people catch me!"

The otter nodded wisely.

Soraya's heart clenched. She didn't like the way Estelle was looking at the otter—with so much trust. If she wanted to keep Estelle's friendship, she would have to get Estelle to look at *her* like that.

"Estelle, I promise, I can help you by myself. The animals can butt out."

"Wishful thinking," said the otter. "We're not going to let a fellow sea creature get turned into a science experiment."

"I'd be fascinating to humans," Estelle said. Her tail flicked. "My scales. My anatomy. My existence."

"We won't let them have you!" said the otter, slapping the ledge of his enclosure. "We'll help."

"We don't *need* their help," cried Soraya.

And then she had a brilliant idea.

"Estelle," she whispered, so the otter couldn't hear, "maybe we don't have to take you to the bay after all."

"What are you talking about?" said Estelle.

"I could sneak you into my house, and you could live in my bathtub."

It was the perfect solution to both their problems. She would rescue Estelle, and then neither she nor Estelle would ever be lonely again.

"You could study architecture as much as you want," Soraya added. "I would bring you lots of books."

Estelle shook her head sadly. "I can't stay, Soraya—I *have* to get back home. I never even got to say goodbye to my family before I got caught in that fishing net. Plus, the merpeople need my inventions. If I don't make it back, they'll live in terrible, collapsing shell-houses forever."

"But if you stay," Soraya said, "no one would think you're weird. *I* don't think you're weird."

"It doesn't matter if my people think I'm weird," Estelle said. "They need me, even if they don't know it yet."

Soraya frowned. Before she could speak, the otter splashed more water at their faces.

"Big crowd coming," he whispered. He dove back down. Soraya saw him rounding up several other otters inside the tank. The otters started catapulting themselves into the air, doing flips as they soared above the walls of their enclosure.

People hurried over to see. The whales had stopped singing, and the visitors in the area were all focused on the otters now. The otters moved away from Estelle and Soraya, trying to get the crowd to follow.

"Ready?" Soraya said. "Hang on." Feeling full of confusion, she dragged the bucket down a hallway and behind another column.

Bartholomew's Request

The column they were hiding behind was right next to the penguins.

"Ugh, penguins stink," said Soraya, holding her nose.

"Don't be so loud, you'll hurt their feelings," whispered Estelle, waving to the birds. They were all waddling up and down the icy paths and hills that had been built for them. Soraya shivered. It was cold at this exhibit.

One of the penguins waddled over and looked down his beak at Soraya. "Bartholomew here," he said in a raspy voice. "What have you done with our fellow sea creature? Trapped her in a rolling box?"

"This is a janitor's bucket," Soraya said through clenched teeth. "And I'm *saving* her."

"Where are you going?" asked Bartholomew.

"Back home," Estelle said.

Just then, a wild, desperate idea started to form in Soraya's head. What if she told Estelle to cover herself with the jacket, so that Estelle wouldn't be able to see where they were going? Then, instead of going to the bay, she could find a way to get back home to her apartment. Once they were there, Estelle would see how fun it would be to live together.

And Soraya would get to keep hanging out with the only person in the world who didn't care that she was weird.

"So what is your plan?" asked Bartholomew.

"The plan is to get me through the entrance hall and out the front doors, and then to the bay," said Estelle. "The bay will take me to the sea."

Soraya said nothing. She would have to figure out a good time to tell Estelle to cover herself with the jacket.

Bartholomew looked toward the entrance hall through a nearby door. "Hmm . . . getting you through the entrance hall will take some planning. I'll make the call for help now." He made some odd screeching noises and slapped his flippers, which the other penguins repeated. For a few minutes, the noises echoed down the hallways. Other animals joined in slapping and calling out, farther away. And then it was quiet.

Bartholomew turned back to them, his eyes wide and hopeful suddenly. "You're heading back to the ocean?"

"Yes," said Estelle.

"Would you consider taking that young fellow with you? It's my son, Paolo."

He pointed his flipper at one of the other penguins.

Soraya stared. "You want us to take your *son*? Don't you like him?" said Soraya. Were all fathers alike?

The penguin's eyes widened. "Of course I love him—that's why I want you to take him." His eyes filled with tears. "I want him to have the chance to see the ocean and have a proper penguin's life. I want him to see the open air, the crashing seas, the cliffs . . ." He stared off into the distance. "All the things *I* never got to see for myself."

"But didn't you come from the ocean?" asked Soraya.

"No, I was born here," Bartholomew said

heavily. "I want my son to have a better life. He deserves to have grand adventures!"

"Dad, are you talking about this again?" Paolo waddled up, shaking his head. "He's always trying to get me to escape," he said to Soraya and Estelle.

Soraya stuck out her bottom lip. "Dads shouldn't be okay with letting their kids go."

"It's true that I'd miss Paolo terribly," said Bartholomew. "But I want him to have the life of a free penguin. He would be happier, and that would make *me* feel happy."

"Dad, stop this." Paolo patted his dad's flipper. "I've *told* you, I'm happy here. I've got you and Mom and my ten aunts and uncles and nineteen cousins. I would miss

you all too much. Maybe I'll be ready to explore the ocean someday, but not right now. Come on, let's go for a swim."

"Wait, son," said Bartholomew, nodding at Estelle and Soraya. "They need our help."

Paolo squeaked excitedly. "Doing what?"

"We need a distraction," said Estelle, "so we can get to the entrance hall without anyone seeing us."

Paolo and Bartholomew exchanged a look. Then Paolo nodded and waddled off as quickly as he could, calling to the other penguins.

Seconds later, something zipped through the air, and then through the water with lightning speed. Paolo and his friends were diving from a little cliff. They popped off the rock like miniature rockets.

Soon all the penguins were shooting off the cliffs, diving like bullets through the water.

"Whoa, check out what they're doing!" said someone in the crowd who was just coming in from the entrance hall.

People gathered around, laughing as the penguins zipped and dived.

Bartholomew looked back at Soraya and Estelle and winked.

"Thanks!" Estelle called.

Soraya grabbed the handle of the janitor's bucket and inched out from behind the column. She waited until no one was looking, and then raced as fast as she could into the entrance hall.

The Stolen Hat

Soraya dove safely behind a towering sign near the front doors, pulling Estelle along with her.

On the sign was a big map of the aquarium. This was their best hiding place yet—the sign was in front of a plant, and they were between the plant and the sign.

"I can't believe we made it this far," Estelle said as she stared longingly out of the glass front doors. "I can't wait to see the bay!"

It wasn't foggy anymore. Sunshine poured into the entrance hall.

Soraya waited a few seconds, then said, "Um, before we run out, you should cover yourself with the jacket. Just in case."

She trembled with guilt, especially when Estelle smiled and nodded. Soraya could see that Estelle trusted her now. She thought of Bartholomew. He had been willing to lose his son just to make sure Paolo was happy, even if it meant never seeing the young penguin again.

She pushed the thought out of her head.

"Okay," said Estelle. "But how will we get past those guards?"

"I don't know." Two guards stood at the doors, watching everyone who came in and left.

"They'll definitely see us." The excitement faded from Estelle's face. She grabbed Soraya's hand. "Soraya, they'll lock me up if they see me.

They'll stick needles in me and hook me up to machines."

"I won't let that happen," said Soraya fiercely. "I *promise*, okay? We'll think of something."

She looked around, her mind racing. There were no animals in the entrance hall, so there was nothing to distract anyone. More people strolled in through the front doors all the time. Some of them wandered right up to the sign and started reading the aquarium map. They didn't realize that anyone was hiding behind it.

Soraya bit her nails. Nimbla Moony would have called Ziggy, the stardust horse, who would have trampled anyone who tried to get in her way.

Soraya closed her eyes. She wished really, really hard for her own magic horse to appear. It didn't even have to be made of stardust. Any kind of magic horse would do.

She opened her eyes. No horse.

"What's wrong?" asked Estelle.

"Nothing."

Just then, a high cawing sound rang through the entrance hall. Soraya looked up. Birds were streaming through the open front doors, gliding up to the ceiling. They called out, filling the whole place with their cries.

"Seagulls!" cried Soraya.

"Yeah!" Estelle smiled up at the birds in wonder. "Remember that Bartholomew said he'd call for help so we could get through the entrance hall? This must be what he meant. He must have sent word through some of the animals who have outdoor exhibits. I can't believe the seagulls came to help us."

The seagulls seemed to be having fun. More and more of them flew into the entrance hall, making a big show of swooping and cawing and wheeling around in midair. Some people laughed and took out their cameras. Others screamed and covered their heads.

One of the gulls dove down, grabbed the hat off a guard's head with its beak, and glided back across the entrance hall. The bird's caws sounded like laughter.

"Give that back!" The guard hopped up and down a few times, then chased after the bird. The seagull flew just low enough that the guard kept jumping up to grab his hat, but couldn't reach it.

The second guard ran behind them, also shouting. Soon, more people in the entrance hall started chasing the gull, too. Other people just hurried away, shrieking and ducking as birds dove low.

"It's an attack! An attack!" yelled one man.

One of the gulls swooped close to Estelle and Soraya's hiding spot.

"What are you waiting for?" the bird said. "*Now*. Go now!"

Soraya hauled the janitor's bucket out from behind the sign, and raced for the exit faster than she'd ever run in her life. Both guards had left the front doors. She burst outside—right into the sunshine.

Just as she stepped out into the light, she heard a woman call out behind her, "Hey, why is that little girl pulling a janitor's bucket?"

"They saw us!" cried Soraya. She raced in a blind panic through the parking lot, stopping to hide behind a parked van.

"Whatever we do, we can't let them see you," she told Estelle, quickly throwing the jacket over the mermaid's head to make sure she was completely hidden.

She looked around desperately. The sidewalk on the other side of the parking lot led in two directions. To the left was the bay. To the right was the way to Soraya's house.

Soraya thought and thought. She wasn't sure she could find the way home by herself. It was a long way. But if she made it, they could be friends forever. Soraya would never let anyone hurt Estelle.

Because you weren't *supposed* to let people go. Soraya's dad had let her go, and that felt horrible. She wanted to hold on to Estelle and her friendship forever.

What would Nimbla Moony do? she asked herself.

And then she realized something. Not once in all the *Nimbla Moony* books had Nimbla ever had to worry about something like this. Because even though Nimbla's friends lived all over the galaxy, Ziggy, the magic horse, could take her to visit them in seconds. So Nimbla never really had to say goodbye.

Soraya stood there, stumped. Nimbla *always*

had an answer. The idea of Nimbla not having an answer was impossible to imagine.

You didn't want *your dad to let you go*, a little voice in Soraya's head said. *But Estelle* wants *to go back to the sea. What people want matters.* At that moment, Soraya's heart hurt.

Estelle wiggled under the jacket. "What's going on?" came her muffled voice. "Why are we stopped?"

A few grown-ups came out of the aquarium. "She must be here somewhere," one shouted.

Soraya made a decision. Her whole body felt heavy with sadness. She pulled Estelle out of the parking lot and rolled her along the sidewalk behind a row of tall bushes. The plants blocked the view from the aquarium.

She heard more shouting behind her, but she didn't look back. She raced the squeaky bucket down the block and toward the crosswalk. It led to the park across the street, which sat right at the edge of the bay.

Latitude and Longitude

Nimbla Moony would have created a crystal bridge over the traffic. Nimbla never had to worry about honking cars or traffic lights or annoying things like that.

People in passing cars looked at Soraya strangely, but she didn't pause. The crosswalk light turned. Soraya ran across the street, dragging Estelle behind her.

"Hang on!" She dashed into the park, down a little grassy hill, and up to the bay.

Nearby, a man sat on a bench, reading a book. A few kids flew a kite far down in the park's grass. No one was looking at them.

She wheeled Estelle around so they were hidden behind a leafy bush near the water.

"Hurry, hurry," she said, yanking the jacket off Estelle. The people from the aquarium would come looking for her soon, she was sure of it. "We don't have much time."

Estelle's eyes lit up when she saw the bay. "We're *here*! You did it!"

"Seriously, we have to hurry." Soraya turned the bucket on its side and dumped Estelle right into the bay.

The second Estelle slipped into the water, Soraya felt as if she could breathe again. Estelle was safe. She could hide. She could swim away. No one was going to experiment on her.

Estelle was under the water for a second, then leapt out again joyfully. Soraya kneeled at the edge of the water and smiled, even though she felt like her heart was breaking.

"You did it, you really pulled it off!" Estelle cried, doing a flip.

"Be *quiet*," said Soraya, wiping her eyes. "I don't want those people to hear you."

"Which people?" said Estelle.

"The aquarium people. They saw us leave. I think they're coming."

Soraya wiped her eyes again.

"What's wrong?" said Estelle, swimming closer.

Soraya looked down. "Okay, I'll tell you. Promise not to hate me?"

"I promise," said Estelle, her eyes wide.

"I almost didn't bring you here," Soraya admitted. "I was going to sneak you home and stick you in my bathtub."

Estelle stared at her. Then she laughed. "I'm really glad you didn't do that. I don't even know what a bathtub is."

"If you shrink down a pool so it's tiny, that's a bathtub."

"Then I'm *really* glad you didn't do that," said Estelle.

"I lied about something else, too," Soraya added, her face turning red. "You know how I said I'm popular? I'm not. No one likes me. They think I'm super weird."

Estelle looked puzzled. "*Some* of them think weird is good, right? *I* think weird is good."

"I know. That's why I want you to stay!" Soraya exclaimed. "You'd like me if you stay with me, I promise. I'm not like—like . . ."

"Like what?"

"Like my dad thought I was. I promise. I'm not like that. You'll see. I could find you a better place to live than my bathtub. And that way you'd have a friend."

"Gregory is my friend," said Estelle, looking up with shining eyes, her tail swishing. "And now you're my friend. I have two friends." She patted Soraya's hand. "I need to go back."

Soraya paused. "But I'll be far away, if you go back home," she whispered.

"Well, if you become a marine biologist, you can dive deep and find me again," said Estelle.

"A marine biologist?" said Soraya.

"They're scientists who study the ocean. Some of them have come *really* close to my kingdom."

Soraya took a deep breath. "I don't know if I want to be a marine biologist. I might want

to become—I might want to be a comic book artist." She lifted her chin.

She'd never said that out loud before.

"That's great!" said Estelle. "Anyway, you can still learn to dive," she added. "And by the time you visit, I'll have a whole new city built for you to see." She lowered her voice. "Do you think you can remember some numbers, if I tell them to you?"

"I can try," said Soraya.

"Okay. Try *hard*, it's important. Listen: 17.7500° N, 142.5000° E." Estelle made Soraya repeat the numbers a few times. "Do you have them memorized?"

Soraya nodded. "What are they?"

"A latitude and longitude," said Estelle. "Coordinates on a map. It's a way to find me again, if you dive deep. Write them down as soon as you can, so you don't forget."

Soraya nodded again, heavily. She looked out at the wide glittering bay. "Are you sure you'll be all right?"

"Yes." Estelle's face was radiant. "And what about you? Promise you'll remember that not everyone thinks weird is bad."

Soraya smiled. "That's what my mom always says, too."

Just then Estelle's eyes went wide as she looked at something over Soraya's shoulder.

Soraya turned. The people from the aquarium were crossing the street to the park. One of them was the guard missing a hat.

Soraya whirled back around to Estelle. "Go. Quick! And stay under!"

But Estelle was already gone, her shining fins hidden somewhere under the water.

Soraya's heart skipped. Estelle was gone. It was as if the bay had swallowed her up.

"Hey!" cried a voice behind her. "Are you Soraya? The girl missing from Ms. Staples' class?"

Soraya stood up and turned around. The people from the aquarium had almost reached her.

Soraya froze. Nimbla Moony would have used her bubble cape to make the janitor's bucket invisible.

Soraya couldn't do that. Instead, she grabbed the bucket and started wheeling it back toward the aquarium.

She raised her chin and walked right past the surprised grown-ups.

"What were you doing?" sputtered the hatless guard. "Did you take that bucket from the aquarium? That's stolen property."

"I'm bringing it back now," Soraya said calmly, still walking.

"But what were you *doing* with it?" cried one of the women. "You gave your teacher such a scare. She was about to call the police!"

"I was having an adventure," said Soraya. "With, uh, this amazing, one-of-a-kind bucket."

"Was there someone with you? A lady at the aquarium said she saw a *child* inside this bucket."

Soraya shook her head. "Nope. Just me. I was *pretending* there was someone in the bucket."

The adults looked at one another with raised eyebrows. Soraya knew what they were thinking: *This kid's poor teacher.*

For once, Soraya didn't care. She turned and looked back at the bay.

Far in the distance, a small figure gave a joyful leap, flipped in the sun, and splashed back down.

"What was that?" said the guard, squinting out at the water.

"Nothing," said Soraya, spinning around quickly. She kept walking as her heart swelled up with pride. Finally, she had been the hero who saved the day. With a little help from some friends, that is.

Come to think of it, her adventure with Estelle was giving her an excellent idea for the first issue of a new comic book series. Soraya couldn't wait to get home and start drawing.

ILLUSTRATOR,
SORAYA AND THE MERMAID

ILLUSTRATOR,
"ESTELLE'S JOURNEY"

Salima Alikhan

has been a writer and illustrator for fourteen years. She lives in Austin, Texas, where she is also a college English and creative writing professor. When she went on school field trips as a child, she liked to imagine what sorts of creatures might be lurking in some of those fun places. She wrote stories and drew pictures about those creatures, and loves that she still gets to do that.

Atieh Sohrabi

was born and raised in Tehran, Iran, and currently lives in New York City with her family. She started her career in industrial design before switching to a new path in illustrations. Her first illustrated book, published in 2002, received first prize in the 5th Tehran International Biennale Illustration. Since then, her books have appeared in exhibitions and museums around the world, winning numerous international awards.

Jennifer Naalchigar

is an illustrator based in Hertfordshire, England. She has a love for quirky characters and funny stories and enjoys experimenting with digital brushes. Jen can often be found doodling with her tablet in her local coffee shop. She also enjoys reading picture books to her daughter. She works in children's and educational publishing and particularly enjoys projects featuring adventurous and clever heroines, just like Estelle!